This book belongs to a little chick called:

_____

_____

Your name goes here

To Sebastian, the third little penguin,
with love from Aunty Gem. GC

To Little Christopher, who walks like
a penguin and whom I call 'Ti'Chri'. DC

North Parade Publishing Ltd

4 North Parade | Bath UK | BA1 1LF
+44(0) 1225 310107
www.nppbooks.co.uk

Two Little Penguins

Written by Gemma Cary
Illustrated by Delia Ciccarelli

Two little penguins lived in their lovely icy home with their mummy and daddy.

Bo was actually not-so-little any more, while his baby sister, Layla, was really quite little.

Although Bo had wanted a brother at first, he had since decided that having a sister wasn't **too** bad, after all. The worst thing was that she followed him... **everywhere!**

Layla followed Bo to school.
Then she followed him home again.
She followed him to the skate park.

And she followed him home again.

Layla was also **very good** at copying her big brother.
When Bo stretched his wings, Layla stretched hers.

If Bo yawned, Layla pretended to yawn too.
Sometimes it was quite **annoying**.

"Layla, **STOP COPYING ME!**" said Bo.

But Layla just smiled.

"Why does Layla copy me **all the time?**" Bo asked Mama.

"Because you're her big brother, which makes you her hero," said Mama.

"Really?" said Bo.

"Yes," said Mama. "Layla learns new things every day, just by copying you."

"Cool!" said Bo, and he started to think about all of the **amazing** things he could teach Layla.

"I could teach Layla how to fish!" said Bo.

"Well, she's not quite big enough for that yet," said Mama.

"Can I teach her how to swim?"

"One day," said Mama. "But not yet."

"Oh," said Bo, and he thought a bit more.

"**I know!** I'll teach Layla how to **talk**."

"**Brilliant idea!**" said Mama.

The next day, at breakfast time, Bo took a fish and set it down at Layla's feet.

"Fish," said Bo. "Yum, yum!"

Layla gobbled up the fish.

"**Dada!**" she said with a great big grin.

"Not quite," said Bo.

Next, Bo took Layla to the Ice Hole, where the
bigger penguins were taking turns to jump into the water.
"Look, Layla – ice!" he said, stamping on the ice.
"Water!" he said, pointing to the water.
Layla looked at the ice and then at the water.
"Dada!" she said happily.

Later, Bo tried **again**.
"Look, Layla," he said patiently.
"**That's** Dada." And he pointed
at their daddy.
Layla looked up. "Dada," she said.

"Yes," nodded Bo, then he pointed to their mummy.
"Now say Mama."
Layla looked at Mama and beamed.
"Dada," she said proudly.

Bo sighed. "I **give up,**" he said.

"What about Bo?" said Mama.
"Can Layla say Bo?"
Layla opened her mouth and
gave a **great**
big
...yawn.

Mama laughed.
"Time for two little penguins
to go to bed," she said.

"It's **impossible**," Bo told Mama that night. "Layla won't copy a **single thing** I say. All she says is 'Dada'."

Mama smiled. "It'll come," she said. And she gave Bo an extra **big** goodnight kiss.

Bo was so tired from his day of teaching that he fell asleep **super** quickly. He dreamed about diving into a great sparkling ocean.

Meanwhile, Layla couldn't sleep. She toddled over to Bo and knelt down. She tapped him gently on the wing and said something very, **very** quietly next to his head.

"**Bo**," whispered Layla.

"Bo, Bo, Bo."

But Bo was swimming in his ocean, chasing fish.

Layla nestled in next to her big brother.
Soon there were two little penguins,
both fast asleep.

goodnight, Layla!